"...It may be thought that the memory of things may be lost with us. We nevertheless have methods of transmitting from father to son an account of all these things...."

Kanickhungo, Iroquois

To Red Thunder Eagle,
who lifts others on his wings, so they can sing.
C.R.

This edition published in 2001.

Copyright © 1996 by The Rourke Corporation, Inc.
Text copyright © 1996 by Gloria Dominic.
Illustrations copyright © 1996 by Charles Reasoner.

Published by Troll Communications L.L.C.

Published by arrangement with The Rourke Corporation, Inc.

First paperback edition published 1998.

Printed in the United States of America.

10 9 8 7 6 5 4 3

Library of Congress Cataloging-in-Publication Data

Dominic, Gloria, 1950-
        Song of the Hermit Thrush: an Iroquois Legend/by Gloria Dominic.
        p. cm.—(Native American Lore and Legends)
        Includes bibliographical references.
        Summary: The animals and birds of the forest hold a contest to choose which will sing a song
to greet the day.
        ISBN 0-86593-428-2 (lib. bdg.)   ISBN 0-8167-4510-2 (pbk.)
        1. Iroquois Indians—Folklore.   2. Tales—New York (State).
3. Tales—Ontario. [1. Iroquois Indians—Folklore.   2. Indians of North America—Folklore.
3. Folklore—North America.]   I. Title.   II. Series.
E99.I7D59   1996
398.2'09747—dc20   96-5113
                                                                                       CIP
                                                                                       AC

Designed by Susan and Dave Albers

■ NATIVE AMERICAN LORE & LEGENDS ■

SONG OF THE HERMIT THRUSH

AN IROQUOIS LEGEND

ADAPTED AND RETOLD BY GLORIA DOMINIC

ILLUSTRATED BY CHARLES REASONER

Troll

One bright morning, Dancing Flower and her little brother Dark Eyes walked with their grandmother in the forest looking for berries.

"Listen to the birds," said Dancing Flower. "They sing so loudly!"

"Yes," agreed Grandmother. "It is their morning song."

Dancing Flower and her brother looked at one another, smiling. They knew from Grandmother's voice that a story was coming. They waited expectantly.

"The song you hear now is very different from the one we hear at dusk," said Grandmother. "I will tell you why this is so."

Long, long ago, the birds and other animals came to live in the forest. In order to live peacefully together, the animals made an agreement.

"Let us divide the forest," said Bear. "That way there will be enough room for all of us. Birds, you are used to flying through the air. So it makes sense for you to live high above the ground in the trees of the forest."

Bear pointed to the beavers, turtles, snakes, and other animals. "The rest of us are creatures of the land. We will live on the ground, where we are most comfortable."

The birds agreed. Things went well for a while. But, every day at sunrise, there was a problem. Each morning, as the creatures of the forest awoke, there was an awful sound.

Awwwk! Scrawwk! Grrrowwwl! From the trees came the screeching and squawking of the birds. From the ground came the growls and bellows of the other animals.

Bear called a meeting. "What is the meaning of this loud noise each day?" he asked.

"We are grateful for the sunrise," explained an elk.

"We wish to praise the day," added a pretty red bird.

The animals agreed that a song to give thanks for the day was a good idea. But the sound of their voices calling out together was not beautiful to hear.

The animals decided to have a contest. Each one would have a chance to sing a song to praise the day. Then all the animals would choose which song was the best.

Moose began. He bellowed.
It was a loud sound, but not a lovely one.

Turtle tried next.
He snapped his jaws.

It was a proud sound,
but not a beautiful one.

Raccoon cried out in her shrill voice.

Coyote howled and yowled.

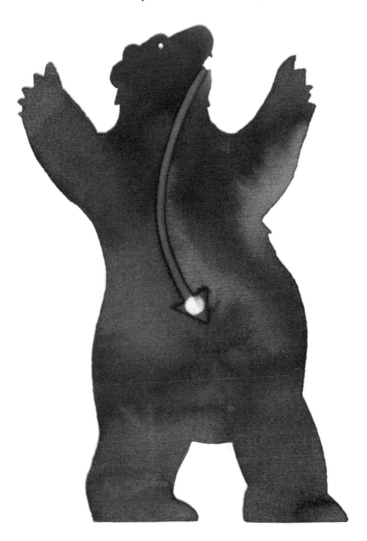

Bear growled.
No one could sing sweetly.

"Enough," said the red bird to the ground animals. "You have had many chances. Now let us try."

One by one, the birds sang their songs. Some could sing sweetly, and some could not. But the birds and ground animals agreed that not even the prettiest song was good enough to praise the day.

"Where can we find a proper song?" the red bird asked.

"That is easy," said Owl. "The sweetest of all songs is found high in the sky where the Great Spirit lives. That is where we will find the best song."

"Easier said than done," replied the red bird. "The home of the Great Spirit is high above the clouds. None of us has ever flown there before."

"Surely we should try," said another.

"*Caw-caw! You* try," said Crow, who knew she did not have a very good singing voice.

"I will try," said Hawk. "I am strong, and I like to fly high."

Hawk spread his wings. He flew and flew. But soon he grew tired. He looked up and saw the white clouds waiting above him. They looked so far away! Hawk gave up and turned back to earth.

"Let me try," said Goose. She took off proudly, beating her wide wings. Before long, though, she also returned. "I am too heavy to fly so high," she admitted.

Many birds tried, but no one could reach the sky high above the clouds. At last, all the birds went to Eagle.

"Eagle, you are the strongest," said one.

"Your eyes are the sharpest," said another. "Surely you can reach the Great Spirit's home."

"I am strong," said Eagle. "But I like a wild and rough life. I am not a songbird."

"Please try," pleaded the other birds. "Then all will know that you succeeded where others failed."

If there was one thing Eagle loved, it was a challenge. His bright eyes lit up. "Yes, I will go," he said.

As he spread his powerful wings and took off, Eagle did not feel a small bird hop upon his back. The dull brown color of the little bird blended in with Eagle's dark feathers. Unseen, the little bird watched the earth grow small as Eagle rose into the sky.

The bird hung on quietly as the fluffy white clouds grew closer. He was very impressed with Eagle's great strength, as they climbed nearer and nearer to the Great Spirit's home.

"Soon we will climb above the clouds," the brown bird thought. "Then I will hear the sweetest of all songs!"

Just then, Eagle said, "What fine clouds you are! How beautifully you float in the sky! I'll bet I can float just as well as you!"

Eagle swooped gracefully among the clouds. This way and that he looped and played, floating perfectly. "Just as I thought, I can do it!" he said triumphantly.

The little brown bird did not share Eagle's excitement at this new trick. "Why is he wasting his strength when we still have so far to go?" he wondered impatiently.

Finally Eagle grew tired of his game and continued to climb. Now they were above the clouds. "The home of the Great Spirit can't be far away now!" the brown bird told himself.

Suddenly, Eagle turned back to earth. "I am too tired to fly any farther," he said. "I must rest and have something to eat."

The little bird knew what he must do. As gracefully as he had hopped onto Eagle's back, he now hopped off.

"I will not give up!" he cried. Flapping his small wings, he flew nearer and nearer to the Great Spirit. His long rest upon Eagle's back served him well, for he found the strength to finish the journey.

Soon sweet sounds greeted his ears and bright lights met his eyes. The little bird had arrived at the home of the Great Spirit. "The stories were true," said the bird. "These *are* the sweetest songs."

The music of this place was so beautiful, he could not stop listening. Softly, he sang each of the songs he heard.

At last, he heard a melody so perfect, he knew it was the sweetest song of all. He listened closely. Then he sang the song again and again, until he knew it by heart.

The small bird did not want to go, but he knew he must return to the forest with his prize. But as he flew back to earth, the bird began to worry.

"What if Eagle is angry with me?" he said. "What if the other animals are jealous of my song?"

When he finally reached the earth, the little bird did not announce his triumphant journey. Instead he found a dark place in the forest, a spot overgrown with vines and bushes. There he hid until the sun began to set.

When he heard the other birds and animals settling down for the night, the little bird grew brave. "Now they are too tired to chase after me," he said. "Now I will sing."

The bird came out of his hiding place and found a perch in a tree. Then he threw back his head and sang. Out came the sweetest song of all. He had remembered it perfectly.

"So, children," said Grandmother with a smile, "to this day, at sunrise, you may hear the noise of the birds and animals as they awake and greet the day. At that time, the forest is a noisy and busy place. For although the creatures have never discovered how to sing the best song, they continue to try.

"But at dusk, listen closely. As the sun goes down and the forest grows quiet, you will hear a lovely sound. It is the hermit thrush singing—all by himself—the sweetest song he knows."

The Iroquois

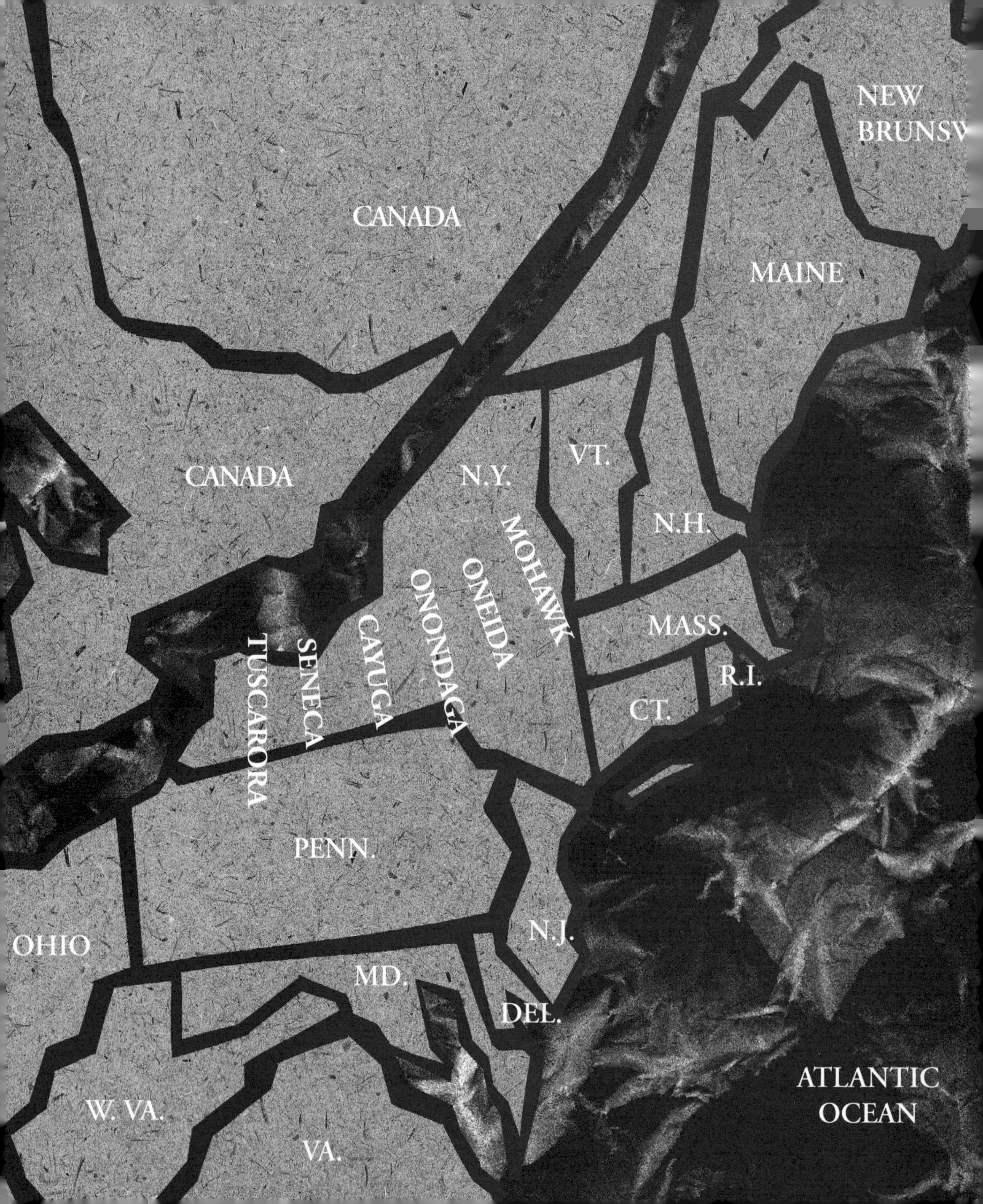

NEW
BRUNSW
CANADA
MAINE
CANADA
N.Y.
VT.
N.H.
MOHAWK
ONEIDA
ONONDAGA
CAYUGA
SENECA
TUSCARORA
MASS.
R.I.
CT.
PENN.
N.J.
OHIO
MD.
DEL.
W. VA.
VA.
ATLANTIC
OCEAN

THE IROQUOIS

Iroquois Homeland

The Iroquois homeland stretched across present-day New York State. Rich in resources, the area provided everything the Iroquois needed: lush woodlands abundant in trees for housing, canoes, fuel, and tools; animals for food and clothing; plants for food and medicines; and lots of fertile land for planting crops. Lakes, rivers, and marshes provided fresh water, fish and game.

Many related families lived together in longhouses. Built using a framework of poles tied together then covered with sheets of bark, these rectangular structures had straight sides, arched or slanted roofs, and the clan symbol carved over the entrance. They were weatherproof and as long as 200 feet! Each longhouse had a center hallway that held the cooking fires. Each side of the longhouse was divided into open compartments that sheltered individual families. Each compartment shared a cooking fire with the one across the aisle.

Villages consisted of twelve or more longhouses protected by a surrounding trench and palisade, or wall of stakes driven into the ground. Villages were often built near rivers, with crops located outside the palisade.

This is what an Iroquois longhouse looks like.

Iroquois People

"Iroquois" comes from "Hilokoa," a word from rival Algonquians meaning "Killer People." They called themselves "The People of the Longhouse." They are a large society made up of six groups: Cayuga, Mohawk, Oneida, Onondaga, Seneca and Tuscarora.

Before the 1500s, they were constantly at war. Legend says two men, Deganawida and Hiawatha (or Hayenwatha), persuaded the chiefs to form the Great League of Peace. (Originally only five nations belonged; the Tuscaroras joined later.) White men called it the League of Six Nations. The Iroquois called it the Brethren, or Brotherhood, of the Longhouse. They saw themselves living in a metaphorical longhouse: Mohawks were the Keepers of the Eastern Door; Senecas were the Keepers of the Western Door; and in the center lived the Onondagas, the Keepers of the Central Fire, the site of confederacy meetings. Many believe the confederacy influenced our forefathers as they formed the government of the United States.

The Iroquois were hunters and farmers, and their lives revolved around the seasons. Men made canoes, houses, and tools; fought wars; and protected the village. Women were responsible for household affairs and raising children. Children were taught by encouragement, examples and stories, and were rarely punished.

A Mohawk girl dressed for her performance at the Pan-American Exposition in 1910.

However, life wasn't all work. Many festivals and celebrations meant singing, dancing and games, including lacrosse. This game was played with a hard ball and sticks with netting or webbing at one end. Sometimes whole villages competed against each other.

As in other Native societies, women held a powerful position. They owned longhouses, controlled the land, chose the chief—and were even able to remove him. Families related on the mother's side lived in the same house and could trace their line to one female ancestor. This type of kinship is called matrilineal. These groups of related people were called clans, and they were named after animals, with the oldest woman as the leader, or clan mother. Children belonged to their mother's clan, and when a man married, he lived with his wife's clan.

Iroquois Nations Council meeting around 1910. Chief David John, Sr. is seated in the center holding the tribal wampum string.

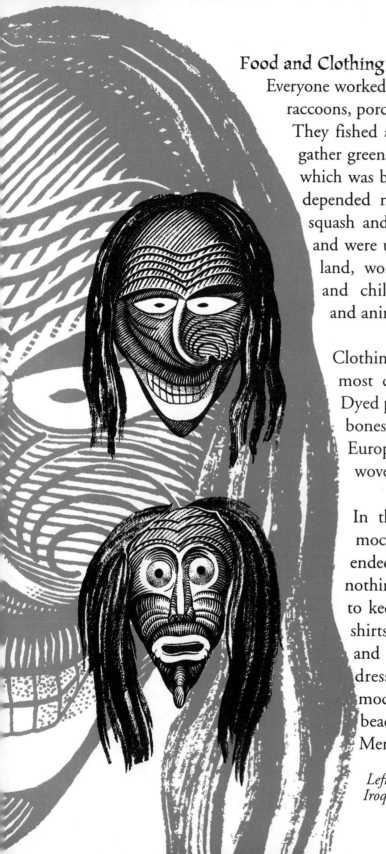

Food and Clothing

Everyone worked hard to provide food. Men hunted deer, raccoons, porcupines, rabbits, turkey, ducks, and geese. They fished and gathered shellfish. Everyone helped gather greens, berries, nuts, wild rice and maple sap, which was boiled into syrup in the spring. But they depended mainly on their crops for food. Corn, squash and beans were called "The Three Sisters" and were usually grown together. Men cleared the land, women planted and cared for the crops, and children helped by keeping away birds and animals.

Clothing was made from animal skins, the most common being deer (called buckskin). Dyed porcupine quills, moose hair, shell beads, bones and feathers were used for decorations. Europeans introduced glass beads, silver and woven cloth.

In the summer, men wore loincloths and moccasins, women wore belted dresses that ended at the knee, and younger children wore nothing at all. In winter, everyone used furs to keep warm. Both men and women added shirts and leggings that tied around the legs and the waist. Women also wore longer dresses. They all wore richly decorated moccasins and jewelry made of silver, glass beads, shells and other natural materials. Men tattooed their bodies and faces.

Left. By wearing masks during sacred rituals, the Iroquois became known as the false face people.

Above. An example of an ornamental comb worn by the Senecas, carved from bone, antler, or wood.

Right. Wampum belts were once used as money and as a sign of sincerity in peace negotiations. But their value was and is more spiritual and personal.

Iroquois Today

Today many Iroquois people live in cities and towns, though some continue to live on reservations in the United States and Canada. The Iroquois confederacy headquarters are at the Onondaga Reservation, outside of Syracuse, New York.

Like other nations, the Iroquois are experiencing an explosion of interest in the traditional ways. Many work recreating traditional crafts, while some follow careers such as doctors, lawyers, and writers. Mohawks have earned a reputation as ironworkers since the 1880s. They have helped build most of the well-known bridges and buildings in the United States and Canada.

A beautifully carved war club.

Above. Moccasins like these were worn by Iroquois people.

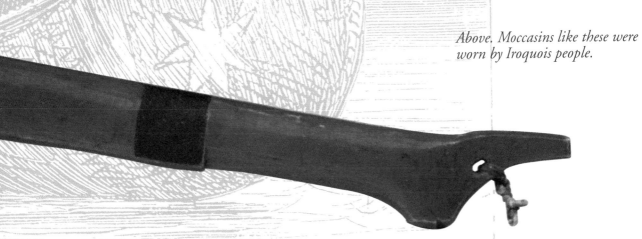

Above. Snowshoes made winter hunting much easier for Iroquois hunters, who could travel up to 50 miles a day wearing snowshoes in deep snow. Iroquois also wore snowshoes in ritual dances.

Right. Short-handled goal-keeper's racquet. It was the Iroquois version of the sport that gave rise to the lacrosse we know today.

Opposite Page. Snare for small birds was made of bark. Corn bait was used to entice a bird to put its head through the hole, and as the bird tried to escape, the noose would tighten.

Glossary

Buckskin: The skin of deer, used to make clothing

Clan: A group of related people

The Good Word: A religion created in 1799 by a Seneca named Handsome Lake, who preached avoidance of alcohol, strengthening of family ties, and farming. Also called the New Religion

Lacrosse: A game played with a hard ball and sticks with netting or webbing at one end

Longhouse: Long, rectangular houses built to house many families

Matrilineal: Tracing descent through the female line

Moieties: Half-nations or tribes

Three Sisters: Corn, squash and beans

Wampum: Beads made from shells and used for money, decoration, and communication

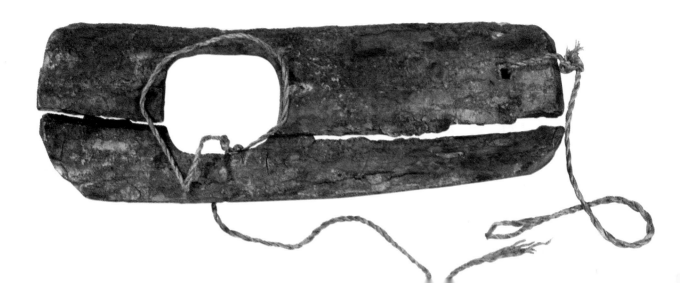

Important Dates

1492: Columbus lands in the Americas

Early 1500s: The Iroquois League is formed

1534: French explorer Jacques Cartier sails through Iroquois territory, opening up the trade routes between the Iroquois and the French

1649: The Iroquois win decades of fighting with the Hurons and become the most powerful Native American group in the Northeast fur trade

1722: Tuscaroras join the Iroquois Confederacy

1776: United States declares independence from Britain. The six nations support different sides

1784: The Iroquois sign over much of their land to the United States in the Treaty of Fort Stanwix, after U.S. Major General John Sullivan led a retaliatory attack destroying Iroquois land and morale. This effectively ends their power in the Northeast

1924: All Native Americans born in U.S. are declared citizens

1927: Clinton Rickard founds the Indian Defense League of America

1968: Indian Civil Rights Act gives Native Americans the right to govern themselves on their reservations

1988: U.S. Congress passes resolutions formally acknowledging "the contribution of the Iroquois Confederacy of Nations to the development of the U.S. Constitution"

1988, 1989: Sacred wampum belts are returned to the Six Nations from the National Museum of the American Indian and the New York State Museum

Using a hollowed-out tree trunk, a Seneca woman named Julia Scrogg makes cornmeal in 1910.

PHOTO CREDITS

Pages 32-33: Forest, Photo by Dave Albers
Hiawatha in Canoe, North Wind Picture Archives, Alfred, ME

Pages 34-35: Map, Illustrated by Dave Albers
Longhouse, Illustrated by Dave Albers

Pages 36-37: Mohawk girl, National Anthropological Archives/Smithsonian, Washington, DC, Neg. 77-5
Iroquois Nations Council, Rochester Museum & Science Center, Rochester, NY, RM 1355

Pages 38-39: Masks, Dover Books
Seneca Comb, Rochester Museum & Science Center, Rochester, NY, RM 2932
Wampum Belt, Dover Books

Pages 40-41: War Club, Courtesy of the New York State Museum, Albany, NY, Morgan Collection, Neg. 36715
Hiawatha in Canoe, North Wind Picture Archives, Alfred, ME
Moccasins, Courtesy of the New York State Museum, Albany, NY, Neg. 37157

Pages 42-43: Lacrosse Racquet, Lacrosse Foundation, Baltimore, MD
Snowshoes, Photo by Dave Albers, Courtesy of a Private Collection
Bird Snare, Courtesy of the New York State Museum, Albany, NY, Morgan Collection, Neg. 36682

Page 45: Seneca Woman, Rochester Museum & Science Center, Rochester, NY, RM 1621

Page 47: Hermit Thrush, Photo by Peter LaTourrette, Los Altos, CA

IROQUOIS BIBLIOGRAPHY

Bleeker, Sonia. Indians of the Long House: The Story of the Iroquois. New York: William Morrow & Co., 1950.

Brandon, Alvin M. The American Heritage Book of Indians. New York: American Heritage Publishing Co., Inc., 1961.

Calloway, Colin G. Indians of the Northeast. New York: Facts on File, 1991.

Doherty, Craig, and Katherine Doherty. The Iroquois. New York: Franklin Watts, 1989.

Editors of Time-Life Books. Realm of the Iroquois. Alexandria, VA: Time-Life Books, 1993.

Robbins, Mari Lu. Native Americans. Huntington Beach, CA: Teacher Crafted Materials, Inc., 1994.

Sherrow, Victoria. The Iroquois Indians. New York: Chelsea House Publishers, 1992.

Snow, Dean. The Iroquois. Cambridge: Blackwell Publishers, 1994.

Waldman, Carl. Encyclopedia of North American Tribes. New York: Facts on File, 1988.